THEM THAT ASK NO QUESTIONS

A SUSSEX STEAMPUNK TALE

BY
NILS NISSE VISSER

DEDICATED TO THE MEMORY OF
MARTHA GUNN, QUEEN OF THE
DIPPERS.

CONTENTS

Free Traders drink

O' the Frenchman's wine

And the darkest night is Owling time

The Aero Fleet prowls the moonless sky

Ashore there be Rozzers on the pry

Yarr! It's a Free Trader's life for me

Riding the clouds like an outlaw free.

BRIGHTON, TUESDAY FEBRUARY 7TH, 1871

Alice missed the small fishing village where she had lived before Mum had been forced to move from Rottingdean to Brighton. That had been two years ago. They all lived in Aunt Beth's little ramshackle house on Artillery Street now, in the sprawling slum called The Lanes. The area was shaped like a long, narrow rectangle, tucked away between the elegant wealth of the seafront residences and hotels on one side, and broad upmarket shopping streets on the other sides.

Shouting a cheerful goodbye to Mum and Aunt Beth, Alice opened the dilapidated front door and stepped out onto the narrow street. She shut the door quickly because it was bitterly cold and the tiny house was barely heated. They had a small stove in the single ground floor room. There were hearths in the small bedrooms on the top floor, but these were never lit because fuel was expensive.

Braving the icy breeze, Alice walked resolutely up Artillery Street. The eleven-year-old girl was barefoot and wore a wide old frayed black dress, a smudged apron, a threadbare woollen shawl, and a battered old black top hat.

Alice had found the hat discarded along the seafront and had been delighted that it had fit her perfectly. She had tied a length of scrap fabric around it in imitation of the popular FlightFunk fashion, since FlightFunkers decorated their hats with scarves, feathers, goggles, and trinkets.

The cold was more bearable because Alice didn't expect to be out in it for very long. She had two errands to run. Both were on the wrong side of the law, so it was best to get them over and done with quickly.

The first job was the reason Alice was cradling a wrought-iron soup pot in her arms, wrapped in a woollen blanket. She was grateful for the warmth that radiated from her delivery.

The Lanes were a maze of narrow streets, twittens, and mews[1], but Alice knew her way around well enough. She made her way to North Street instead of picking a direct route, keeping a wary eye out for possible trouble.

---

[1] Twittens and mews: alleyways and courtyards. Broad Sussex idiom. Still in use today.

Life in The Lanes was invariably interesting for an inquisitive young mind. It was just that there was so much of life, all around, all the time – it was noisy and never-ending. Back in Rottingdean, Alice had been able to escape from it all by strolling up the hills around the village.

Or ask Dad for a ride! …he'd take me cloud chasing in the sky...

Alice scowled fiercely. Dad was dead. Had been these last two years and no amount of wishful thinking was going to bring him back. Better not think about it, or she'd just feel miserable again.

"You're not a child anymore," she muttered to herself.

A few years ago, she had used to play make-belief games with her friend Brax back in Rottingdean. There was no time for that in Brighton. Life had been reduced to a mad scramble for survival. Helping Mum and Aunt Beth raise the weekly rent and food money. Trying to stay a step ahead of the dosshouse, or worse, the workhouse.

Nearing the edge of The Lanes, Alice continued to be vigilant. Although outwardly calm, she was all tense inside, ready to react instantly if need be. There was nothing out of the ordinary though, other than the usual scenes of small human tragedies. A few loud and gin-fuelled domestic arguments from the hovels. Someone's unceasing, racking cough behind closed shutters. The notorious Lanes chavvy Nickie

Nimble-Fingers racing by, pursued by an angry, red-faced police constable.

Small children ran about outside playing tag. They screamed and laughed, ignoring the cold. They evaded a couple of staggering drunken sailors on shore leave. The children seemed oblivious to the groans and squeals from the darker twittens, where street girls serviced off-duty airmen, sailors, and soldiers, as well as gentlemen who had come 'slumming'.

Alice squeezed past such a copulating couple in a murky twitten before emerging right onto North Street, with its imposing facades and elegant shops. An entirely different world, but one that held its own dangers.

Alice's detour via North Street made it easier for her to spot if she was being shadowed by anyone, but she also liked coming here.

A good look at the sky in The Lanes required taking to the roof tops. North Street was broad enough for a wider vista of the wild blue yonder, and she usually spotted aerocraft plying their way to and from Hollingbury Aeroport.

Alice also liked to marvel at the mono-rail that stretched out on its steel pillars along North Street. Especially when an engine hauling carriages, all suspended below the rails, puffed by on its way to Hove, or in the other direction toward the transit station at Old Steine, where passengers could catch connecting services to Kemp Town or the Aeroport.

The mono-rail had street level competition from horse-drawn coaches and carriages, steam-powered lorries and buses, and numerous three-wheeled lektrishaws from the Volk Workshops. There were a lot of people on the pavements, including many genteel couples – who had probably fled inland from the seafront. The broad seaside promenades, as well as the piers and groynes jutting out from the beaches, would be unbearable on a day like this, the icy wind blowing right through everything like a cold, sharp knife.

There were also many uniforms on display, officers from all different services. Alice glared at them. Anyone in a uniform was a Rozzer[2]. She hated Rozzers with a fierce intensity. Rozzers had murdered her father.

Alice walked in the direction of Old Steine. She occasionally lingered by shop windows, seemingly staring at the fancy goods on display in childlike wonder, but actually glancing about discreetly to see if she'd been followed out of The Lanes. She had to do so quickly. If she stayed by a shop window too long, chances were shop assistants would come outside with a broom to chase her away. Lanesfolk weren't welcome either in or outside the posh shops.

---

2 Rozzer: Free Trader's jargon for uniformed representatives of the authorities.

Alice had discovered that getting whacked by a broomstick was no joke soon after moving to Brighton. It was not something to be tried when cradling a heavy soup pot. Nor when a dress was so weighed down by... –additions– ...that movement was funny because it was all just a little bit different than what Alice was used to. She liked to run, but right now it was better not to run at all until her second job was done.

A portly matron opened the door of a bakery and stepped outside with her purchases. Alice came to an abrupt halt, to relish the warm waft of air and delicious scent of freshly baked bread. She breathed in as deeply as she could; hoping that tasting the scent might make her feel less hungry. It didn't of course; it only made her tummy rumble and her mouth water. Still, the smell had been lovely. Alice couldn't remember the last time they'd had proper bread, instead of the old and dry stuff that was the best they could afford at home.

She hurried on but was soon distracted by the sight of an elegant young couple strolling towards her. They were adherents of FlightFunk, with feathered and goggled hats, their winter coats bedecked with wings, cogs, gears, and other outlandish accessories. The scarves flowing from the lady's goggled top hat were multi-coloured and made of fine silk, lifting on the breeze like wings. Alice stopped to stare in frank admiration.

Some said that FlightFunk wasn't real, that its followers just liked playing at being aeronauts. That didn't make sense to Alice. Small children might play at make-belief, but she was sure it wasn't something adults did, unless they were actors on a stage in the music halls or play houses. Why would these two people pretend to be aeronauts? They looked so handsome and dashing; they'd have a fine aeroship waiting for them, surely. Maybe they even lived in it, travelling around the world to chase the endless horizon.

Alice sighed dreamily. Dad hadn't only taken her up into the sky to explore the clouds, but also taught Alice how to skirr a small sky-skiff by herself. The sense of freedom offered by the skies had been exhilarating. She missed skirring *The Liddle Mew*. Since coming to Brighton, it sometimes seemed that she could hear the wind whispering her name as if the clouds were calling her home.

Alice didn't look the part, but wasn't she a bit of an aeronaut herself? Just like these two splendidly dressed aviators?

The lady spotted Alice staring at her. Alice smiled a small greeting. They were fellow aeronauts after all, otherwise she wouldn't have dared. She also gave her head a light shake, to try to lodge loose the scrap of fabric bound around her hat. It had gotten itself entangled in the strings of her apron again; too coarse to dance the breeze in easy elegance like the lady's silk scarves.

"Geoffrey," the lady addressed her companion, alarm in her voice. "That child unsettles me, the way she stares." She clutched her purse tighter.

The man gave Alice an unfriendly look. "Shoo. Go back where you belong. Go on! Shoo!"

He raised his polished cane and swiped it at Alice. It was only a half-hearted effort, easily evaded. Alice dodged past the couple, holding on to her delivery tightly. She threw a wary look over her shoulder in case the gentleman tried to hit her again. Gentlemen's canes were even less pleasant than broomsticks, she knew from painful experience.

"Was it really necessary to strike out at the girl?" The lady asked her companion.

"Yes, my dear," he answered. "The 'vicious classes' are base savages who live like animals. There's no civilised discourse, no appealing to reason. There's only one language they understand."

Alice flinched as he raised his cane and swung it across his path, but he wasn't turning around to come after her, just demonstrating his sparring skills.

"This one was just a child–," The lady's voice faded as Alice put distance between herself and the couple.

The last Alice heard was the beginning of the man's reply: "Worse than the adults. Lost to a life of vice and crime before they can walk. Don't let their tender looks fool you…"

Alice shrugged, pretending indifference. She recalled what was concealed beneath her wide dress and grinned. There was no point in denying some of the things the man had said.

Alice ducked into a dark twitten to weave her way back into the heart of The Lanes. It wasn't long before she encountered trouble.

A tall, bulky man was lumbering her way. Dressed fancy, like a Toff, but his moustache ends were disordered, and he was unsteady on his feet as if he'd been drinking heavily.

Alice squeezed herself into a bricked-up arched doorway, looking down to avoid eye contact, trying not to move at all.

The irregular fall of the man's feet on the cobbles stopped. The man mumbled something incoherent, then spoke up, slurring his words a little as he addressed Alice. "Yesh. You'll do."

He had come to a halt in front of Alice. She shifted the bundle in her arms so that its weight was supported by her right arm. She wished she wasn't carrying the heavy soup pot. It would have been far easier to get away without it.

She looked at the man's face. It was round and sweaty. He was squinting at her through partially blood-shot eyes. He said again, "You'll do."

Alice's heart was pounding loudly but she tried to remain as calm as she could. She replied, "Quiddy?[3] I don't understand, Guv."

"DO NOT!" He thundered in a sudden outburst of anger. "Presume to play games with me, you little bitch. You know damn well what I want."

He was faster than Alice anticipated, shoving out one hand against her shoulder to thrust her back against the rough brick wall. Grinning, he leaned back and started to fumble with his breeches. "Go on," he said. "I haven't got much time. Lift your skirts."

"I don't do that!" Alice protested.

The man barked a laugh. "I bet you've been ridden up against the wall more times than I can count. You slum girls are all the same."

"I told you I don't do that. I'm only eleven!"

"Jolly good." He leered at her. "Let's see what you got."

He abandoned his attempt to open his breeches and reached out for her with his fat sweaty hands and stubby fingers.

---

[3] Quiddy: Derived from the French 'Que Dis Tu', 'What did you say?' Broad Sussex idiom.

Quick as a flash, Alice reached for her hat. She found the finger grip of one of her two hatpins and drew it out, all nine inches of sharp-tipped and glinting steel. She drove it into the pudgy hand fumbling at her chest as hard as she could, breaking skin with ease and driving the point deep down, before quickly drawing it back.

The man howled at the sudden stinging pain and staggered backwards, clutching his bleeding hand.

Now!

The man was momentarily stunned by pain and surprise, but soon his fury would far outweigh any pain he felt. Alice held on to the soup pot as tightly as she could with just her right arm. Her other arm was coiled and ready to strike, her fist closed around the hatpin grip. Alice darted to her left.

"You little savage rat! Vermin!" The man roared and twisted his bulk to intercept her. His arms flailed out at where he thought she'd be, but Alice had immediately reversed her direction when she saw him respond to her feint. She stepped past him on his other side. When she was behind him, she jabbed the hatpin into the back of his leg.

Yelping, the man spun round, reaching for his hurt leg. Like a dog chasing its own tail he turned around again, giving Alice ample time to hide the hatpin in the folds of her dress and then scurry away.

"Come back!" He hollered. "Come back here, you little savage bitch!"

Come back? Alice rolled her eyes as she hurried deeper into The Lanes. She wasn't stupid, was she? Savage maybe, but not stupid.

When she realised the man wasn't in pursuit, Alice slowed down, but only a little. She was near her first destination now and just wanted her outing to be over and done with, to be back home – safe.

It wasn't the first time one of the 'slumming' gentlemen had assumed Alice was fair game because it wasn't uncommon. Alice knew girls as young as nine who plied the twittens. The prettiest ones were sold to the upmarket brothels by their parents. Sacrificed so that siblings could eat – for a while at least.

The encounter had left Alice a little shaken nonetheless. It was always vile. There was also a gnawing ominous thought she couldn't banish out of her mind: That one of these days she might not be able to outwit such a predator.

Throwing last looks all around, determining that it was as safe as could be, Alice sneaked into a small mews. The far wall was made up by a mechanical workshop, its large doors closed and padlocked, the windows shuttered. On either side of the small courtyard were ramshackle wooden shacks, the most abysmal dosshouses in The Lanes. Empty now, they would fill up with dossers later: People without fixed abode lucky enough to have earned a few pennies today, so that they could afford to sleep in one of the narrow, coffin-like beds with straw sack mattresses. Or else, propped up on a bench, with a rope across their chest to prevent them from sliding off. Alice was all too aware that she might well end up in such a place if they failed to make the rent. It was a constant fear.

Refuse from the workshop littered the mews. Alice stepped around a pile of bulky crates. A rat scampered away. There was a man on the ground behind the crates. He was shivering beneath a flimsy blanket and mumbling incoherently. Alice wasn't sure if he was awake or drifting in feverish dreams.

She kept a careful distance. The man had been a Rozzer and sometimes woke up thinking he was fighting in one of the battles he'd been in, roaring fury and lashing out, eyes wild and body as tense as a spring.

"*Mus*[4] Morran," she called softly, setting her blanket-wrapped bundle on the ground. It was a relief to shed the weight, but Alice shivered as she immediately missed its warmth. "*Mus* Morran."

"Huh! What?" Tom Morran jerked upright, looking around him in bewilderment. His face was gaunt, cheeks covered in stubble, and the greying hair on his head an unkempt wilderness.

The meagre blanket that had covered him slid off his shoulders, to reveal a threadbare and much patched army tunic that had once been red, but was now coloured hues of dirty browns.

Initially, Alice had hated the man because of his Rozzerness, bringing him food only because Mum had told her to do so. Once she had got to know Tom Morran a little better she had forgiven him for having been a Rozzer. He was a friendly man, just very confused at times.

"*Mus* Morran. It's just me. Alice." She started parting blanket from soup pot.

"Alice!" Recognition dawned on his face. "Sent by heaven."

"No. Mum sent me, *Mus* Morran," Alice said. She held up the blanket, still warm. "With an extra blanket and hot soup."

"Well then, Clara must be an Angel. Just like her clever daughter."

---

[4] Mus: Mister. Broad Sussex idiom

"Yarr." Alice smiled. She liked that he had said 'clever'. Most men would have said 'pretty'. Most adults seemed incapable of realising that children could be clever at all for that matter, something Alice didn't like because she considered herself to be very clever indeed. Most of the time, anyway, sometimes she forgot to be clever.

"Here, fold this blanket around you first," Alice told him. "It's warm from the soup."

Tom Morran shed the flimsy blanket, shivering. Alice helped him wrap the blanket she had brought around his shoulders, because he barely had the strength to raise his arms.

Alice had sown various discreet pockets into her dress, like the one she had deposited the steel hatpin in. She drew a tin spoon from another such pocket and opened the lid of the soup pot. The soup was still steaming, enveloping Alice in a mouth-watering smell that made her tummy rumble loudly.

Dipping the spoon into the soup, she said. "Mum's best soup. Especially for you, *Mus* Morran."

She started spoon-feeding him the soup.

"Bettermost soup," he said in between spoonfuls. "You must thank your mum for me. Did you know that you look just like she did, when she was your age?"

Alice smiled. He always said that. Mum and Tom Morran had grown up together in The Lanes. Childhood friendship was special, she reckoned. She had made a few new friends in the Lanes, including her best friend Lottie, but Alice still missed Brax. She should go to Rottingdean some time soon to visit him.

If she did, she would go and see Uncle Yard as well, she decided. He had been one of dad's friends and had worked hard to keep the village on its feet after the brutal raid.

That night the Rozzers had come to Rottingdean with a thousand men, wearing red coats, blue coats, green coats, purple coats. They had brought hundreds of muskets, as well as anti-aeroship cannons and Gatling guns. Alice and Brax had cowered beneath a blanket, hidden in a shed behind Uncle Yard's cottage. The cannons had thundered, hurling shells at incoming village aerocraft, including the one captained by Alice's father. The cannons had been joined by the Gatling guns, stuttering their deadly hail at the crews on the wind-chaser *The Salty Mew* and the sky-skiff *The Chameleon*. Both aerocraft had been downed, the survivors finished off by Rozzer musketry.

It wasn't just Dad who had died that night. The village had lost a dozen good men.

Husbands. Fathers. Sons. Brothers. Sweethearts. Breadwinners.

Those who had lost a breadwinner in the raid were immediately unable to pay their rents, including Alice's mum. Uncle Yard had moved heaven and earth to help out. Rottingdean's Free Trader Collective had been hit hard. They had lost half their aerocraft, as well as most of their best Owlers[5]. Moreover, the Rozzers had established a permanent garrison of the hated Queen's Men, the militant arm of Customs & Excise.

By a stroke of luck, the tunnels below the village had remained undiscovered. The Rozzers had been ordered to search all the houses after the killing was done. They had used the opportunity to ransack the houses and steal the villagers' meagre possessions, including Alice's dainty doll from France. Though much was taken, none of the secret entrances were discovered, leaving the Free Traders in possession of a hoard of tea, lace, tobacco, gin, and brandywine.

The first owling activities, conducted under the very noses of the Queen's Men, had consisted of shipping almost all their stock to Lunnon through the Weald. Uncle Yard had used the income to help the bereaved families. But the money had started running out faster than it was replenished. It would take time to re-establish Rottingdean as a viable Free Trading partner, and it had been made harder by the day all along the Sussex and Kent coasts. The Royal Navy had sent warships to reinforce the Coast Guard cutters on sea. The Royal Aero Fleet had been deployed to support the Coast Guard aerocutters in

---

[5] Owlers/to go owling: smugglers/to go smuggling. Free Trader jargon.

the sky. The army had started running fire-trains on the lines between Worthing, Brighton, Eastbourne, Hastings, and Rye. Dragoons had patrolled the Downs in force, as had the yeoman cavalry.

None-the-less, Rottingdean's Free Traders had revived because Sussex wunt be druv[6]. Sussex folk had been Free Trading for over five hundred years, and, proud of being stubborn as pigs, viewed new obstacles as challenges to be overcome. The revival in Rottingdean was only recent though, after years of struggle. Too late for the families who had lost a breadwinner. The landlords, in a collective display of the power of the moneyed classes, had raised all the rents in Rottingdean as further punishment. Many families had suffered the indignity of eviction, moving to slums, dosshouses, or Brighton's workhouses – Rottingdean's community torn asunder.

I want to skirr again.

Continuing to spoon-feed Morran, Alice decided that she would ask Uncle Yard for work. She was good enough to crew and he knew it. He'd object, of course, and Mum would look sad.

"I've lost a good man to Free Trading," she often told Alice. "Must I lose my daughter as well?"

Alice recalled the drunken, red-faced fat man and felt a shiver crawl along her spine. She would ask

---

[6] Wunt be druv: Won't be pushed around, won't be driven. Broad Sussex idiom.

both Mum and Uncle Yard outright if they would prefer her to ply the twittens to earn a living, hoisting her skirts against rough brick walls. Uncle Yard would be shocked. Mum resigned. In the end, Alice could make decent wages doing what she longed to do with mind, body, and soul – chasing clouds high up in the sky…away from vile menfolk on the ground.

Lost in her thoughts as she was, Alice was entirely unaware of the men who walked into the mews until one of them spoke.

"Here she is!"

Alice spun her head around to look.

ROZZERS!

Alice jumped to her feet, backing away from Tom Morran and glaring at the two blue-coated and helmeted police constables who blocked the only way out of the mews. The younger constable, with an open, gullible face, pointed at her. "You're nicked, girl."

"Hold your horses, Constable Cuffins," the older Rozzer said. He had a roguish look about him and was looking at Alice thoughtfully. "How do you know this is the girl? What description did the gentleman give?"

"He said he was assaulted by a little savage in a dress and a battered hat, Constable Harding."

"I didn't assault nobody!" Alice protested.

The older Rozzer called Harding ignored her, shrugging at his colleague instead. "The Lanes are populated by hundreds of little savages in dresses. A fair few larger ones as well."

"We could search her," the man called Cuffins suggested. "And know soon enough."

"No!" Alice shouted.

If they searched her, they'd find…everything.

Harding shrugged. "If it's a slum job, there'd be more than one chavvy involved. First to swarm the mark, and then to break up in all directions, passing the swag from one to the other. I expect it'll be far gone already."

Tom Morran broke into fit of coughing.

Cuffins peered around the crates. "She's been feeding a vagabond! Soup!" He gave Alice a triumphant look. "Caught red-handed, Missy."

He looked at the older Rozzer. "Constable Harding, we can apprehend her for violating the Vagrancy Act[7]. Take her back to the station, lock her in a cell and sort out the rest at our leisure."

No!

Alice braced herself, ready to put up a struggle.

Harding shook his head. "You'd condemn a chavvy to a month of hard labour at Lewes[8]? Just because she was feeding some poor bugger soup?" He peered around the crates, and frowned when he

---

[7] Vagrancy Act (1824): begging or rough sleeping was an offence that could lead to fines or arrest and subsequent detention in prison or a workhouse, as was aiding and abetting a homeless person. The Vagrancy Act is still in effect today in the UK and used by some councils to force homeless people to pay a fine for the 'crime' of being homeless or threaten to arrest those feeding the homeless.

[8] Lewis Prison. Up until 1899, children sentenced to prison sentences were often locked up in adult prisons.

saw Tom Morran, still sitting upright, but swaying and with his eyes closed. "Well I'll be…"

Harding turned to his younger colleague. "Cuffins. The Chief isn't far. Go find him, ask him to come as quick as he can."

Chief? Alice's eyes widened. *Chief Forty-Guts? The Chief Constable?*

"But…"

"Do it. Now."

Cuffins made off.

Alice regarded the remaining Rozzer warily.

Harding hadn't been all bad for a Rozzer, not eager to nick her for feeding a hungry man like that younger one was. Yet, there was a cleverness about him that unsettled Alice. She reckoned he'd be hard to outwit.

She eyed the long police whistle clipped to his blue coat, further attached by a steel chain that looped into the coat. They were within a whistle blow of the police station. Even if she got away, that whistle would have The Lanes crawling with Rozzers within moments.

Alice tried her best innocent smile on Harding, but it didn't change his demeanour.

"You're the Gunn girl." He said. "Artillery Street. Clara Gunn's daughter."

Alice stared at him without giving an answer. His words had been a double blow. It was bad news that the Rozzer knew who she was and where she lived. It made running pointless, unless she left Brighton altogether. On top of that, Alice was still mightily upset that Mum had opted to revert to her maiden surname, experiencing it as a betrayal of Dad.

She wanted to correct the Rozzer, tell him her name was Alice Kittyhawk and not Alice Gunn. She didn't because she figured it wasn't clever to let a Rozzer know she shared a surname with the most notorious smuggler ever to skirr the Sussex coast.

"Fine, don't answer." Harding shrugged. "Suit yourself. Just know that I was born and bred in these here Lanes before I joined the army. No funny business, savvy? I know all the tricks in the book, and a damned few you haven't even thought of yet."

"I weren't planning nothing," Alice lied. "I'm innocent!"

Harding laughed. "As innocent as a lamb, I'm sure. Why don't you feed Tom the rest of the soup? Be a shame to let it go to waste and he looks like he needs it. Aside that, it'll keep you busy."

Tom? He called Mus Morran: Tom.

Alice regarded the Rozzer suspiciously. "All-along-of it being unlawful. The Fragrant-Sea Act, bain't it? I'm a good girl. Innocent. I don't fancy a stint in the quarries up at Lewes, do I?"

"Less of your cheek, Miss Gunn. Do I really need to spell out just how much trouble you're in?"

Alice didn't answer.

Harding took a few steps backwards so that the crates blocked his view of Tom Morran. "Just feed him the soup. Me eyes are shut, me ears are closed, me nose is plugged, and me lips are sealed. May they remain ever so if I lie to you."

It was an impressive pledge, not bad for an adult, and a Rozzer at that.

Tom Morran stirred, coughing again. Alice turned her attention to him, feeding him the rest of the soup.

She had a good notion of the amount of trouble she was in. Alice now figured that it had been a mistake to pick the fat gammon-faced man's pocket when he spun around again and again, all his attention focused on his pain. She hadn't been able to resist the temptation of such an easy prize and struck immediately after tucking the hatpin away. There had been no chance to examine the wallet yet, but it had felt wonderfully bulky when she had slipped it under her dress. Except now the Rozzers were looking for the wallet.

If they found it, they would find everything else as well. Punishment for that would make a month's hard labour in Lewes seem like a fancy Sunday picnic on Hove Lawns.

The soup was finished. As Alice placed the lid back on the pot, she could hear a heavy footfall on the cobbles. The ominous sound was joined by the outraged voice of Constable Cuffins.

"Aiding and abetting idle and disorderly persons, sir! In violation of the Vagrancy Act. We caught her red-handed."

"You saw the girl feed the vagabond soup?" A deep booming voice filled the mews.

Alice flinched and made herself small, still out of sight behind the crates. Everything indicated that the Chief Constable of Brighton had just arrived. The top Rozzer himself, commonly known as Chief Forty-Guts because of his ballooning girth.

"Well…no, sir," Cuffins answered. "There was the vagabond, the girl near him with a spoon in her hand, and a pot of soup atween them."

"That bain't red-handed," the booming voice mused. "Spoon-handed, mayhap, but that bain't breaking any law I ken."

"But, sir!"

Alice crept to the edge of the crates for a cautious peek. It was Chief Forty-Guts alright, towering in the centre of the mews, his blue coat with four lines of tin buttons bulging around his middle, huge silver sideburns concealing his jowls, and a bowler hat on top of his head. He was in his sixties and made a formidable impression that emphasized his reputation as a Rozzer not to mess with.

"Begging your pardon, Sarge," Harding announced.

Why is he calling the chief 'Sarge'?

Harding continued. "But young Cuffins here may have been overzealous again. We got a vagabond, a fierce scrap of a girl, a spoon, a cooking pot, but no…"

"No soup?" Chief Forty-Guts guessed.

"No soup." Harding confirmed. "Cooking pot is empty. May have contained soup. Smells of it. Good soup too. But no soup in there now, Sarge."

Alice realised just how clever Harding had been, though she was puzzled as to why a Rozzer would want to be that helpful.

The chief turned to Cuffins. "Seems to me, Constable Cuffins, that you lack a vital piece of evidence."

"Evidence?"

Alice grinned at the young Rozzer's puzzled face.

"Evidence, Constable Cuffins," the chief explained. "An important aspect of police work. It might be an idea to re-read your training manual."

"But, but…" Cuffins stammered.

"No buts," Chief Forty-Guts said gruffly. "We'll not be arresting folk for exercising Christian charity. Not on my watch. I don't care what Lunnon[9] says, it don't come right to me[10]. Savvy? Well done, Harding.

---

9 Lunnon: London. Broad Sussex idiom
10 "It don't come right to me" was Housing Activist Harry Cowley's battle cry between the World Wars, here given earlier roots

Now where is this hardened and vicious, but charitable criminal of yours?"

"Miss Gunn," Harding called out. "The Chief Constable requests your presence."

"One of the Gunns, is she?" Chief Forty-Guts asked.

"Aye, Sarge. Fancies herself a regular little Robin Hood, robbing the rich, feeding the poor."

Figuring she had no choice, Alice stepped into view, still holding the spoon and scowling at the Rozzers. "My name bain't Gunn nor Robin Hood, and I'm innocent cause I bain't robbed no one."

The chief raised his eyebrows. "Innocent?"

"Yarr! I'd like to go home now, Guv. Me mum'll be worried."

"You're not going anywhere just yet." Chief Forty-Guts informed her. "Cuffins. There was another small matter, wasn't there?"

"Yes, Chief Constable," Cuffins confirmed eagerly, but then fell into a silence.

"Well, spit it out man." Chief Forty-Guts frowned. "What allegations were made?"

"Huh, yes, sir. Sorry, sir. The gentleman…"

Alice snorted.

"…said he was on his way to a meeting, thinking to take a short-cut, when out of no where and unprovoked, a savage girl wearing a battered hat assaulted him and then robbed him."

"Serious allegations." Chief Forty-Guts spoke slowly, looking Alice directly in the eyes. "A serious crime. Gallows. Noose. A young girl such as yourself may be too light for her neck to break when the trapdoor opens. Choking. Kicking. Gasping for breath that won't come. It bain't the bettermost way to go, if you ask me."

Alice averted her eyes. She had the uncomfortable feeling that Chief Forty-Guts could look right into her mind and read her thoughts. The Rozzer's words struck home, and she hated and feared him with equal intensity.

"Assault and robbery," Chief Forty-Guts mused.

"That's what the gentleman said," Cuffins confirmed.

"Did you think to question his story, Cuffins?"

"Question, sir?"

The Chief sighed. "Can you describe the gentleman? How big was he?"

"He was a big man, tall, 5'8, maybe 5'9. But–"

"And you mean to tell me this snoule drib[11] of a girl here, fierce as she may be, 'assaulted' a man four or five times her size? It don't come right to me."

Harding sniggered.

"He's a gentleman, sir." Cuffins frowned. "Them don't lie. Unlike these Lanesfolk, every other word what comes out of their mouth is a lie. He said

---

[11] Snoule & drib: a small amount of anything, and a very small quantity. Broad Sussex idiom

she had a knife. He was bleeding, sir! He said the little savage held him at knife-point, and then stabbed him in the hand and in the leg."

"He's a liar!" Alice howled angrily. "I didn't assault no one. I'm innocent! I don't even have a knife, I used me hatpin, didn't I?"

"Used your hatpin for what?" Chief Forty-Guts asked.

Alice bit her lip; it hadn't been clever to tell him about the hatpin.

"I don't know nothing about no robbing," she insisted. "Honest, Guv. And I don't have a knife. Just me hatpin. Look!" Alice plucked her second hatpin from her hat. It was a flimsy affair made of copper. Already bent, it looked like it would buckle at the slightest hint of resistance.

Harding laughed.

"Held up at knife-point indeed," Chief Forty-Guts rumbled. "Yet, you drew blood, girl. Why in the blazes would you be doing that, if not to–"

"It were his own fault!" Alice said angrily. "He should have kept his big fat hands to himself, bain't it? I told him I were no street girl. But he pressed me against the wall and started...he wanted...he started...So I jabbed me hatpin at his hand, maybe his leg, I don't remember. I was frightened!"

Cuffins looked shocked. "How dare you accuse..."

"Harding?" Chief Forty-Guts growled.

"The gentleman in question," Harding said. "Has a reputation for…his preferred tastes."

"Why didn't you tell us straight away?" Chief Forty-Guts challenged Alice.

"Who would have believed me?" Alice retorted. "My word against a gent's?"

"Zackly!" Cuffins exclaimed.

"The little wildcat has a point there, Sarge," Harding said.

"Alice?" Tom Morran's voice, weakly from behind the crates. "Alice?"

She looked his way, instinctively responding to her name. Another mistake.

"Alice is it?" Chief Forty-Guts glanced at the crates which blocked his view of Tom Morran. "And what is your surname, Alice?"

Alice kept her mouth tightly shut.

"I see," Chief Forty-Guts mused. "Them that ask no questions…"

Isn't told a lie. Alice's mind completed the proverb automatically. It was Free Trader's jargon. She narrowed her eyes. Why was the Chief Constable using Free Trader talk? Smuggling talk? She became acutely aware of the extra weight evenly distributed around her dress. Did he know?

"…isn't told a lie." Chief Forty-Guts continued. "Well, Alice, despite your reluctance to reveal your surname, I'm of a mind that your telling of it be more accurate."

Hope soared through Alice, but she kept her face straight. "Yarr, Guv. I'm innocent. I keep telling you, don't I?"

"Sir!" Cuffins protested.

"How old are you, Alice?" Chief Forty-Guts asked.

Alice saw no harm in revealing that. "Eleven, Guv."

"Harding, remind me, what is the legal age of consent again?"

"Twelve, Sarge."[12]

"Motive enough, for the 'gentleman' to deviate from the truth. Don't you think so, Cuffins?"

"If you put it that way, sir."

"I am…and if the gentleman cares to show up at the police station to make enquiries about this investigation, you send him straight to my office, savvy? I'd be happy to tell him what's what."

Alice's eyes widened. She could barely believe that a Rozzer had apparently chosen to believe her words over those of a Toff's.

"But," Chief Forty-Guts continued. "There is still the matter of a missing wallet. If you are as innocent as you claim, Alice, we won't find that wallet anywhere upon your person, will we?"

Alice took several steps back, crouching, holding up the tin spoon in one hand, the dodgy copper

---

[12] Historical. Raised to 13 a few years later in 1875 because so many young girls were being sold to brothels.

hatpin in the other. She hissed, "Nobody's touching me! I don't want your filthy Rozzer hands on me." She bared her teeth at them, her eyes darting left and right. Harding, on one side of the chief, was too clever. Cuffins, on the chief's other side, seemed far less clever, she might be able to –

"ALICE!" Chief Forty-Guts boomed. The sheer volume of his verbal thunder was enough to make Alice freeze. Having captured her full attention, the chief spoke in a gentler tone, his eyes fixed on hers. "Alice. None of us is going to touch you. Do you understand? Alice? We won't touch you."

Alice hissed her disbelief.

Without taking his eyes off her, Chief Forty-Guts addressed Cuffins. "Constable Cuffins. To the nearest hospital, if you please. Fetch a nurse, bring her to the station."

"Yes, sir." Cuffins seemed relieved to make a retreat.

"Alice," Chief Forty-Guts said. "We'll escort you to the police station. A nurse will come and do the search. She can also check to see if you were hurt. We will not be touching you, is that clear?"

Alice nodded slowly. That solved the problem of being manhandled in the mews, buying her a bit more extra time before both wallet and small fortune in smuggled contraband were discovered beneath her dress.

It didn't seem like much of an improvement, but Alice relaxed her body just a little, not having realised until now just how tense she'd been.

That was another mistake.

A big mistake.

Coming out of her crouch, Alice dislodged the wallet which hadn't been as securely stowed away under her dress as she had assumed.

The wallet landed on the cobbles with a loud and leathery thud.

There was a moment of complete silence, as Alice, Chief Forty-Guts, and Constable Harding all stared at the wallet. It was even bulkier than Alice remembered, bulging with bills.

"Now that would be–" Chief Forty-Guts began to say.

"I dunno how that got there, Guv," Alice quickly said, drawing a sardonic laugh from Harding that she rewarded with an angry glare.

"I took it! I took the wallet."

To everyone's surprise, Tom Morran stumbled to Alice's side. He was swaying on his feet, his head lolling, chin on chest. "I took the wallet."

"Don't look to me as if you're in a state to do any such thing." Chief Forty-Guts said.

Tom Morran's swaying got worse, his legs buckling. Alice moved in to support him, urging him to rest an arm on her shoulders so he wouldn't fall over.

"Thank you, Alice," he said, then lifted his face to look straight at Chief Forty-Guts. "Nonetheless, Sergeant Willoughby, I'll stand in front of a judge and swear under oath that I took the wallet."

Sergeant Willoughby?

"HELL'S BELLS!" Chief Forty-Guts exclaimed. "Private Morran? Tom?!"

Morran grinned weakly and gave the chief a wobbly salute. "Present and accounted for, Sergeant Willoughby." He gave Harding a quick nod. "Corporal Harding."

"Private Morran," Harding acknowledged him, before turning to the chief. "Meant to tell you, Sarge. That it were Tom Morran being fed by the little wildcat. But you and Miss Gunn were busy scorsing pleasantries." [13]

Alice looked from one to the other in bewilderment.

"35th Regiment of Foot, Second Battalion," Harding said to her, as if that explained everything.

"Quiddy? Second foot?" Alice looked at her feet, most people had a second foot as far as she was aware. Apart from the ones with just the one foot. Or none at all.

"I didn't know you were back in Brighton, Tom," Chief Forty-Guts said.

---

[13] Scorsing: exchanging. Scorsing pleasantries: extended greetings including idle chit chat and gossip. Broad Sussex idiom.

"I didn't want to bother you with me troubles, Sarge, you being a busy man these days."

"You should have…the others?"

Tom Morran's face fell. "Ben died, Sarge. We went hop picking in Kent, and after that to Lunnon for some dockyard work. Fever got Ben in Lunnon. Rob and Pete are about Brighton, Sarge. Last I heard they were off to Shoreham to see about unloading some coal at the harbour. I got ill, you see, couldn't afford the dosshouse no more. Then it just got worse."

"Sit, sit." Chief Forty-Guts took Morran by the arm and helped him sit on a crate. Harding retrieved the blankets from the cobbles where they had fallen and wrapped them around Morran.

"It's been cold, so cold," Morran said. "But we've been through worse, haven't we, Sarge?"

"Aye, that we have, Private."

"Do you recollect the winter camp at Plabennec?" Harding asked.

"How could I forget?" Chief Forty-Guts shuddered. "I thought the winter would never end."

"The Bloody Battle of Bloody Brittany," Morran said, and they all laughed.

Alice stared at them as if they had gone mad. She decided she didn't mind, they seemed to have forgotten all about her. She glanced down at the wallet on the cobblestones and began to edge toward it as stealthily as she could.

Mayhap…

"I think not, Miss Gunn." Harding reached down and scooped up the wallet, grinning as he rose again.

She made a face. "I weren't…"

"…doing nuffink wrong cause you're as innocent as a choir girl." Harding finished.

Chief Forty-Guts shook his head. "Tom, about this wallet…"

"Sarge, me mind is set. Without Clara and Alice I'd have been dead weeks ago. Nobody else cared. They did, with nothing to gain from it." Morran paused, as if exhausted by speaking. "I got nothing going for me, Sarge. Doubt I'll have long anyways. This one, she's got her whole life ahead of her."

Alice was overwhelmed by his words. "*Mus* Morran…"

"Me mind is set, Alice," he said stubbornly.

Harding let out a low whistle, drawing everyone's attention. Wide-eyed, he opened the wallet for them to see. It was crammed full of bank notes.

Alice stared in astonishment and horror.

Astonishment, because of the denominations on the scores of bank notes. £200. £500. £1000. She had never seen so much money before.

Horror, because it could have been hers. Should have been hers. It seemed more than enough to buy an aerocraft, hire a crew and set up business as a channel-runner. Maybe even get a few silk scarves for her hat.

More horror, because it occurred to her that such a great deal of money meant a severe sentence for sure. She peeked at Tom Morran, stricken by guilt.

Chief Forty-Guts and Constable Harding exchanged a long glance.

The chief held out his hand and Harding handed the wallet over. The chief stuck it in his coat pocket. Alice noticed the little bulge the wallet made as it slid down deep. It'd be hard to retrieve in a casual manner, she concluded with disappointment.

"Evidence," Chief Forty-Guts boomed. He looked at Alice. "That's us done, Alice-with-no-surname."

"Quiddy?"

"You're free to go, Miss Gunn," Harding explained. "We got our culprit, and there was no soup."

"No soup," Chief Forty-Guts confirmed.

"Yarr, because I'm innocent!" Alice sang out triumphantly, but then her face fell. "What about *Mus* Morran? Are you going to stick him in a workhouse? Like the Fragrant-Sea Act says you should? Or send him up to Lewes?"

The chief and Harding did that glancing thing again.

"What we'll do," the chief chuckled. "Is deputise him."

Alice didn't know what 'deputise' meant, but it sounded like a harsh punishment. "You can't! It's not fair!"

"Deputise, Sarge?" Tom Morran asked. "You can do that?"

"*Posse Comitatus*," Chief Forty-Guts said mysteriously. "The 1642 Militia Ordinance."

"The Sarge reads a lot of books, Private Morran," Harding explained.

"As you should, Corp," Chief Forty-Guts reprimanded the constable. He turned to Morran. "Harding will sign you up back at the station, Temporary Constable Morran. You'll be honourably discharged within twenty-four hours, with a day's pay in your pocket. And severance wages."

"And then?" Morran asked. "Why…"

"Then you'll be a retired police officer," Harding tapped the side of his nose.

Alice had lost the plot completely. She looked at the Rozzers suspiciously. "So you're not going to stick him in a workhouse? Or prison?"

Chief Forty-Guts regarded her with amusement and said, "Them that ask no questions…"

Alice frowned at him. That was meant to be used *against* Rozzers, not *by* them.

"Alice," Tom Morran said. "I'll be alright. Leave now, girl, go home to your mum. Count your blessings, eh?"

Alice hesitated. It was hard to believe that she was free to go. She looked at Chief Forty-Guts.

He nodded. "Go cut your stick."

Harding handed her the empty soup pot.

Remembering her second job and realising that Morran was right in reminding her that she'd just crawled through the eye of a needle, Alice turned and scampered.

Alice's dress had loops and hooks sown into the lining. Thick rolls of pressed bacca[14] wrapped tightly in old newspaper coiled round and round, supported by the loops and hooks. It was part of a recent 'crop' transferred from a Dutch freighter to local hogboats and then brought ashore.

After weaving another detour through The Lanes, just in case the Rozzers tried to follow her, Alice announced her presence at a back door of the Old Ship Inn. She was ushered in by a matron, and taken to a small storage room where they began the laborious process of carefully retrieving the coils of bacca.

Alice was only half listening to the matron chatting away. There was much on her mind. The pain of losing the wallet was fading fast. She was used to counting money in terms of farthings,

---

[14] Tobacco

42

ha'pennies, pennies, tuppences, sixpences, and the occasional shilling. Although she recognised a £1000 bank note was worth a fortune, she had no real notion of that amount of money, let alone multiple bank notes with that denomination.

Most of all, her thoughts were on her encounter with the Rozzers in the mews. She hated Rozzers. But these had been…nice, she suspected, in their own way. But by being human, they had made things more complicated, so that was another thing to hate them for. Hating Rozzers was easier. Besides, in the end, they had been cruel. The story of the wallet had just become really interesting when they had suddenly cut her out of it. Now she would never know. They'd probably stick the money in their own pockets, she concluded bitterly.

When at long last her dress was freed of the bacca, the matron tossed a shiny shilling at Alice, who caught the coin deftly. "A bob for your trouble."

"Bethanks!" Alice beamed, and, free to go, started making her way home through The Lanes.

She was pleased to be bringing a shilling home. Mum's face would light up when Alice gave her the gleaming coin. Mum didn't like Alice doing this work but a shilling would make a big difference this week. Tom Morran wasn't the only one. Mum and Aunt Beth were feeding other unfortunate Lanesfolk as well, to keep them from complete starvation. That had brought more folk knocking on the door for help. Times were hard.

Alice's thoughts went back to Tom Morran and the two Rozzers. She was fascinated by the bond between the three men. It had been familiar but she hadn't been able to place it back at the Old Ship Inn. It became clear to her now. It reminded her of a Free Trader crew. It had been the way Dad and his shipmates had behaved, on or off his beloved *Salty Mew*. It was like a second family, Alice supposed.

Alice smiled bravely. Maybe she could think of Dad for a while, without all the other stuff swirling in her mind. Think of him in a nice way and try not to feel miserable. She began to sing softly and kept it up until she reached Artillery Street.

I'd like to see you my love,
With the chavvy on your knee,
But my heart is now with skiff and crew,
Skirring o'er the angry sea,
The bitter-gales, by steam and sail,
The sheltered cove our goal.
It's the wayward life,
It's Free Trader's strife,
It's the joy o' the Owler's soul.

When she reached Artillery Street, Alice turned the corner only to immediately duck behind a parked cart. Her heart was pounding as she dared a peek.

Her front door had a sentry. Constable Harding, whistling a martial tune but keeping a wary look-out. The door swung open and none other than Chief Forty-Guts stepped out of Aunt Beth's little house. He gestured at Harding to follow him and the Rozzers left.

Alice's heart skipped a beat. The sight of the Chief Constable walking out of her house could only mean trouble.

Are they looking for me? They said I could go! Trickery? Am I going to be deputised after all? What have they told Mum?

She had planned to keep her account of the day's business in The Lanes short. She'd stick to the Rozzers catching her feeding soup to Tom Morran, but deciding not to make an issue of it. What if the chief had told Mum she'd stabbed the fat man? Mum would be so disappointed, she disapproved of people stabbing other people. Or maybe he had told Mum about the wallet and that Tom Morran was going to be punished for Alice's crime.

Alice followed the progress of Chief Forty-Guts and Harding down the street. Once they were out of sight, she ran to the house and burst in through the front door.

"Mum?! Aunt Beth?"

Aunt Beth was nowhere to be seen. Mum sat at the table. She was crying. The weight of guilt turned Alice's legs and tummy into lead, sure that this was her fault.

"Mum? What did Chief Forty-Guts do to you?"

Mum shook her head. "No, no, Alice. It's alright. These are different tears." She smiled through her tear-stained face.

It didn't make sense to Alice. "Mum! What did that Rozzer do?"

"Rozzer?"

"Chief Forty-Guts. What did he say? Why did he make you cry?"

"I don't want you calling Ernest a Rozzer, Alice."

"Ernest?"

It was getting more confusing by the minute.

"Ernest Willoughby, the Chief Constable."

"Mum! He's a Rozzer. They killed dad!"

"No." Mum shook her head. "They're not all the same."

Alice had begun to suspect as much, what with Tom Morran, and then the chief and Harding who had sort of appeared to be on her side earlier. She stared at the worn tabletop with a sullen expression.

"Oh, Alice." Mum sighed. "Sit down, we need to talk."

Alice did as Mum asked. She remembered to lay the shiny shilling on the table and pushed it towards Mum. "For running the Black Rock crop."

Mum picked up the coin and dropped it into a pocket of her apron. "Thank you, Alice, that's much needed. About the other thing. The Brighton Constabulary wasn't involved in the Massacre on the Green. There wasn't a copper in the village that night."

"They were soldiers before that! Redcoats! Together with *Mus* Morran. Second Foot something."

"The 35th wasn't involved either," Mum said. "Lunnon has just about enough common sense not to use local regiments. Sussex men might not follow orders if told to shoot at other Sussex men." Mum's voice hardened. "If you want someone to blame, look at the damned officers involved, the ones who made the decisions."

"All right," Alice conceded. "But Chief Forty-Guts is still a copper."

She half expected Mum to tell her not to call the Chief Constable 'Chief Forty-Guts', but Mum didn't.

"You've got too much Kittyhawk in you." Mum sighed. "As stubborn as your father was."

Alice beamed.

"But you have Gunn in you too, Alice."

Alice pulled a face. She'd still rather be Alice Kittyhawk than Alice Gunn.

"It's something to be just as proud of. I suspect your great-great-grandmother Martha Gunn would have recognised you as being of her blood, surely."

"Great Granny Gunn! Queen of the Dippers. I learned a ditty about her," Alice said. She recited:

To Brighton came he,
Came George III's son.
To be bathed in the sea,
By famed Martha Gunn.[15]

Mum laughed. "That would have been scandalous. Prinny[16] didn't come to Brighton until he was twenty-one. They did know each other though. Prinny was fond of Martha and gave her leave to roam the royal kitchens. Did I never tell you how they met?"

Alice shook her head. Part of her wanted to return to the topic of Chief Forty-Guts and why he

---

[15] Old English rhyme, author unknown.
[16] Nickname for George, Prince Regent (1811 to 1820), King George IV (1820-1830).

48

had been in their house and made Mum cry. But she sensed a story coming on and knew Mum well enough to know that the story would have to be told first.

Mum stood up and walked to a cupboard from which she retrieved a small box. Alice cast a curious look at it when Mum placed it on the table. The box was made of dark green cardboard.

"Prinny was very fond of military pageants," Mum said. "He liked to parade the troops, or even have them re-enact famous battles that Wellington fought against Boney's[17] Frenchmen. One day, when Prinny was staying in Brighton…"

"At the Royal Pavilion!"

"It was still the Marine Pavilion then, smaller and less fancy. But yes, he was staying there. He ordered two battalions to march to Brighton. One battalion kept on their red coats. The other was issued blue ones, left over from a theatre production."

"French army coats!"

"Yes. Prinny wanted to stage a French invasion of England. To be beaten back, of course, by heroic redcoats. Right on Brighton's beaches. So when the big day came, Royal Navy ships started ferrying the 'French' troops from brigs and frigates to the beach. Prinny had commandeered the grand balcony of The

---

[17] Boney: Napoleon Bonaparte, French Emperor

Duke's Hotel for him and his guests. Other important people were viewing from The Duke's other balconies, or just on the promenade overlooking the beach. Prinny was in a good mood, chugging down gin from a bucket as if it was lemonade, as he liked to do. But someone had blundered. You see, the battalion of redcoats that was to beat back the bluecoat invasion wasn't local, they didn't know their way around too well."

"They got lost!" Alice laughed.

"Zackly. They got lost, not marching towards the sea front but heading west, on the road to Shoreham. The bluecoats came ashore and organised their ranks, but there wasn't a redcoat to be seen at the top end of the beach. There was much confused shouting, and that led to a new problem. The bluecoat regiment wasn't local either, they were from way up north somewhere."

"Surrey?" Alice guessed[18].

Mum shook her head. "Even farther."

"Lunnon!"

"Many miles to the north of Lunnon."

"There's more north above Lunnon?"

Mum smiled. "A lot of it. This regiment hailed all the way from Northumbria, a far stride from Sussex, surely. Folk speak very differently up there."

---

[18] It's well known in Brighton that "The North" starts just beyond Devil's Dyke, at the edge of the South Downs.

"Like Surrey! They're all chuckle-headed in Surrey, bain't they?"

"I've heard it said, but you'll find the difference in dialect increases the farther you go up north. Back on Brighton beach, Lanesfolk who had come out to watch the spectacle, couldn't make head or tail of all the shouting in the Northumbrian dialect, so they reasoned that the bluecoats must have been French! Panicking, they fled into The Lanes, shouting that the French had landed."

"But they weren't really French, were they?"

"The people in The Lanes didn't know that though. Nobody had thought to tell them. Because Lanesfolk are seen as—"

"—base savages who live like animals," Alice supplied.

Mum raised her eyebrows. "Where'd you hear that?"

"I heard some people say it, this morning on North Street."

Mum sighed. "Yes, well, it's how we're seen. Back then as well, so Lanesfolk had been kept in the dark. In those days, Alice, there had been a real threat of French invasion for a long time. It wasn't at all unrealistic that it might happen. Boney's ambitions knew no limits. So Lanesfolk were ready to believe there were real French soldiers stretching their legs on Brighton's beaches. They were frightened and a great many Lanesfolk gathered in front of Martha Gunn's house on East Street."

"Why would they do that?"

"Martha Gunn was their champion. She was eighty-six or eighty-seven years old then. Still a formidable presence, still working as a dipper. She told the crowd: 'Brighton bain't meant to be a Frog sea resort, it don't come right to me'."

"And then?"

"She ordered the Lanesfolk to arm themselves. It was the time of year that a lot of menfolk were off doing seasonal work elsewhere, so Martha's little army consisted mostly of women and children. They came charging out of The Lanes waving broomsticks and the like. Raced across King's Road and the promenade, then down the steps onto the beach, hollering Martha's name and 'Sussex wun't be druv'!"

Alice laughed as she pictured the scene.

"It's funny," Mum acknowledged. "But also incredibly brave. As far as the Lanesfolk knew, the bluecoats at the bottom of the beach were Boney's men, armed with muskets and bayonets. And still they charged them."

Alice nodded solemnly. It had been brave.

"Those bluecoats, now, only had mock training stocks, not real muskets. They looked like muskets at a distance, but there was no shooting to be done with them. At best they could be used as clubs, but the soldiers didn't want to start beating women and children. They hollered for the Royal Navy sailors to row back and pick them up. When Martha Gunn and her followers reached the bluecoats scrambling to get back on the boats, they gave them a right bannicking[19]. They say Martha Gunn picked an officer up by the scruff of his neck, lifted him in the air and then gave him a knock-out punch, shouting: 'Get thee back to France!'"

Alice laughed. "And Prinny?"

"Prinny was delighted and cheered the Lanesfolk on. Afterwards he asked that Martha be brought to him and that's how they first met. He was much impressed. So much so he had a medal made especially for her, to reward her for 'exceptional civilian valour on the battlefield'."

Mum slid the little box over to Alice. "It's in there. Martha's medal. The only one ever made."

Alice lifted the lid gingerly. Resting on a blue velvet bed, was a beige and turquoise ribbon with a gleaming bronze medallion attached in the shape of an octopus with outstretched arms, four of them entwined around the handle of a broom.

"It's beautiful!" Alice exclaimed.

"So it is." Mum nodded her agreement. "Now, one of the Lanesfolk involved that day was a young lad. Seven, or eight at the time. His parents were

---

[19] Bannicking: beating. Broad Sussex idiom.

drunkards, so the lad was usually left to his own devices."

Alice nodded. She knew plenty like him in The Lanes. Her friend Lottie too. She lived with her aunt and uncle just a few doors down the street, but they were always tossicated[20].

"Martha had taken him under her wing, made sure he had enough to eat and never left out on the streets when it was raining or freezing cold. When she gave the orders to charge what they thought were armed French soldiers, he followed her without hesitation."

"It's what I would have done!" Alice blurted out.

"Charging armed soldiers with nothing but a broomstick in your hands?" Mum asked. "Probably. And I can't even blame your poor dad for that, because that would be the Gunn in you."

Alice grinned.

Mum continued, "A few years later the young boy was sometimes seen transferring 'crops' about Brighton."

"He became a Free Trader!"

"More of an occasional tubman than right in the thick of it like your dad, but yes. That was before the lad joined the army as a drummer boy."

---

[20] Tossicated: intoxicated. Broad Sussex idiom.

"Army?" Alice frowned, suddenly wary of why Mum was telling this story now.

"The 35th. That boy's name was…is Ernest."

"Chief Forty-Guts?! He knew Great Granny Gunn?"

"He worshipped the ground she walked on."

Alice was astonished. Old people were forever telling her that they had been young once, but it was always hard for her to imagine. Especially when it seemed that they had forgotten what it was really like to be young. They usually spoke in terms of carefree swanning about without obligations, seeming to forget all the rules, the confusion, and the sheer frustration of trying to make sense of adults.

The notion that Chief Forty-Guts, as stout and forbidding as Alice imagined the Rock of Gibraltar to be, had not only been a small boy but one of the Lanes chavvies, a Free Trader even…

"Why would a Free Trader become a soldier?" She asked. "And then a copper? He betrayed his own people!"

"Did he betray you, in The Lanes today?" Mum asked sharply.

Alice looked at Mum warily. How much had the chief told her? Fortunately, she could give an honest answer. "No, he didn't."

"I didn't think so," Mum replied.

"Did he come here to tell you all this? About Great Granny Gunn?"

"No, Alice. I knew that already. My grandmother was there as well, at the Battle of the Broomsticks. Not much older than Ernest and waving a broomstick about like a regular Boudicca. She told me all about it when I was your age. As I have just told you."

Alice liked that. If she'd ever have children, she'd tell them the story too. Maybe she could tell Uncle Yard as well. He liked to hear good stories, and often took notes and asked questions. One day, he had once said, he was going to write them all into a proper book, like the stories he used to read to Alice and Brax in his cottage garden.

She asked, "So why did Chief Forty-Guts come here? What did he say?"

Why did he make you cry? Did I make you cry?

"He came to offer employment."

"Employment? Work! Are you going to work for a Ro…a copper?"

"He wants you to work for him as well."

"Me! For the police? NEVER."

"Listen carefully, Alice," Mum said. "The Chief Constable isn't our enemy."

"He arrests people and puts them in prison!"

"He arrests murderers, rapists, burglars, and thieves. And I am glad he does."

"What about the folk sent to the workhouses? Just for having nowhere to stay?"

Mum smiled. "Not a single one of 'em apprehended by the Brighton Constabulary. Chief Willoughby refuses to do so. It's the City Council officers that round people up. I can assure you that the chief hasn't forgotten his humble roots, here in The Lanes. We're his folk, Sussex folk, and he does what he can to protect us from the worst of life. Mayhap, people don't always know what he does because he's a modest man. He doesn't do what he does to get acclaim. I reckon he does it because Martha Gunn was always telling him to do the right thing."

Alice stared at the medal. Chief Forty-Guts had protected her today, she supposed. He could have just thrown in the nick and let some judge deal with her. "I won't call him a Rozzer no more."

"Thank you. That will make it easier, I'm sure."

"Make what easier?"

"He wants to talk to you. At St. Nicholas churchyard. Five o'clock."

"Why? What else did he say about me?"

"He said that you were very brave today. Very brave. 'A regular little trooper' were the words he used." Mum's voice trembled and she smiled with the kind of motherly pride that was a bit embarrassing, even without anyone else there to see it.

"If he thinks he can talk me into becoming a snitch…" Alice crossed her arms. "…he's got another think coming. I bain't going to be chaunting or turn nose. I don't bark or bleat, do I?"

"Your vocabulary hasn't much improved since we moved back to Brighton." Mum sighed.

"You moved 'back', I was never here to begin with. I was born in Rottingdean."

"Oh, I think you'll find that your life started here, in Brighton," Mum said with a mysterious smile. "At any rate, I think you should go talk to the chief. He deserves a fair hearing at the very least. If only because his first battle was one in which he answered your great-great-grandmother's call to arms."

"All right," Alice nodded reluctantly. "I'll go talk to him. For Great Granny Gunn's sake."

"You'd better hurry then, or you'll be late." Mum rose from her seat. "I'll walk with you a while, to the Ferguson's shop, turn some of your Free Trader earnings into a hot meal tonight. But, wait…"

Alice had stood up already, but now waited by her chair. Mum lifted the medal from the little box and pinned it on Alice's dress.

"Mum! That's Great Granny Gunn's!"

"She doesn't need it anymore, bless her soul. She passed it on to my grandmother, who passed it on to me. And all I've done with it, is leave it unseen in a cupboard. I believe that Martha Gunn would have been proud to see you wear it."

Alice glowed with pride and peered down to admire the medal.

"For eggs…" Alice faltered, trying to remember the words.

"Exceptional civilian valour…" Mum supplied.

"Exceptional valour on Brighton beach."

Mum laughed. "On Brighton beach indeed."

There must have been a FlightFunk convention in Brighton, because the intersection between North Street, West Street, and Queen's Road was crowded with feathered and goggled folk. Alice quickly fished her shiny long steel hatpin from its special pocket in her dress and stuck it back in her hat next to the dodgy copper one, to increase her meagre collection of FlightFunk accessories.

Martha Gunn's medal was the best one, of course. Alice was as proud as a peacock and preened a little as she made her way through the FlightFunk throngs.

She tried to make eye contact with the gentlefolk, waving regally at those who noticed her, adding the Free Trader's greeting which she supposed must be universally recognised among aeronauts. "Fair winds to ye. Fair winds!"

Two of the ladies screamed shrilly, as did one of the gentlemen. From the rest there was nothing but shocked revulsion or sheer disapproval.

Alice laughed at them. She didn't care if all these out-of-town visitors looked down on her. She was the great-great-granddaughter of Martha Gunn, Queen of the Dippers, Friend of Prinny, Champion of Lanesfolk, and Victor of the Battle of the Broomsticks. Exceptionally valorous.

There was no reason, she decided, why she couldn't be both Alice Kittyhawk and Alice Gunn.

If Uncle Yard took her on as crew, she'd get a Free Trader's name as well. Free Traders didn't use their own names when they went owling. Dad had been called Cap'n Hawkeye, and sometimes when they had skirred together, they had been Gurt Hawkeye and Liddle Hawkeye[21].

Much as she loved her father though, Alice didn't want to be known as Liddle Hawkeye anymore. She'd think of something else. Something of her own. 'Liddle' was fine when she had been nine, but she was much older now.

Alice left the milling crowds behind and started walking up Dyke Road. As she neared the lower gate of the St Nicholas church grounds, she spotted Harding standing by the gate. Behind him a path climbed steeply through the graveyard, until it

----

[21] Gurt and Liddle: Respectively Great and Little. Broad Sussex idiom.

reached the low, medieval church with its short, squat tower.

"Little Missy Wildcat," Constable Harding greeted her with a wide grin, but tipped the rim of his helmet politely.

Alice frowned at him, then smiled. Mum hadn't said anything about Harding.

"*Mus* Rozzer," she replied, likewise tipping the rim of her top hat.

"Chief's waiting for you." He opened the gate and Alice walked past him.

It didn't take her long to find the Chief Constable because she suspected where he'd be. He was standing with his back to Alice, facing Great Granny Gunn's gravestone, his bowler hat in his hand to reveal his unkempt silver hair.

Alice took her hat off as she came to stand by the chief's side. She tried to read the words on the gravestone, but the only ones her eyes could focus on were:

Martha Gunn

It was cold up here on the hill overlooking Brighton's rooftops, and Alice shivered.

"Miss Alice Gunn," the chief rumbled.

"Chief…Willoughby." The name sounded strange, but Alice could hardly call him Chief Forty-Guts to his face.

He glanced sideways. His owlish eyebrows rose briefly when he saw the medal, but he didn't comment on it.

"Chief?" Alice dared to ask. "*Mus* Morran?"

"Safe, warm, well-fed."

"In a police cell?"

He shrugged. "Better than out in the open in a mews and conveniently available. It's only temporary. The cell door is unlocked. Morran is free to come and go as he pleases."

"So he's not in trouble?" Alice asked, not quite understanding why that would be.

Am I in trouble again?

"Nobody is in trouble," Chief Forty-Guts said with satisfaction. "When we got back to the station, the alleged victim of a vicious robbery was pacing up and down, shouting at my poor constables. I took him aside for a word."

"A word? Are you going to put him in prison?"

The chief looked her in the eye, a sad expression on his face. "I'd like to, Miss Gunn, but I don't know a single judge who would take your word over his."

Alice nodded. "Shame, he belongs in prison."

"That he does," the chief agreed. "Instead, I had to give him back his wallet. But you may be pleased to know that he took it home empty."

"Empty!?" Alice stared at the chief with wide eyes. "You nicked the swag!?"

"By Geemeny!" Chief Forty-Guts looked shocked. "I'm an honest copper, I am."

"Innocent," Alice said.

He grinned. "Zackly. Let's just say that I convinced him to donate every last penny of it to the *Brighton Constabulary Retired Officers' Convalescence Fund.*"

"The what? Convinced? But…how? What did—"

"Them that ask no questions…"

"Isn't told a lie." Alice completed, not bothering to hide her disappointment. She would have liked to know exactly how the chief had 'convinced' the fat man to part with an awful lot of money. She suspected it must have been most amusing. For her, anyway, not for the disgusting gammon-faced Toff.

"Things are moving fast, Miss Gunn. You know that building at the far end of Artillery Street? With the boarded-up doors and windows?"

"Yarr, the old sailmakers."

"I'm buying it. It's to be a convalescence home for retired constables, regular or deputised."

Alice couldn't help herself. "A house full of Rozzers."

"Men like Tom Morran," the chief reminded her.

"I suppose that's different," Alice conceded.

"It is," the chief confirmed. "I'm not sure you'd understand, Alice. Men like Morran, they risked their all for Queen and country. They followed me into battle dunnamany[22] times, without hesitation, without question."

"Like you followed my Great Granny Gunn?"

The chief looked puzzled for a moment, then nodded, a smile on his face. "Zackly. Just so. Except folk got hurt badly in the wars. Some died, some came back missing arms or legs, or blinded. It don't come right to me that the country they suffered for is happy to discard them, leaving them to fend for themselves on the streets. So we're setting up a fund, to pay for upkeep of the building, food and drink, beds, blankets, clean clothes—wages for staff."

"Staff! Mum?"

"And your auntie. The bettermost folk I can think of, to take care of the likes of Morran. And doing so for decent weekly wages, no more scrounging about for the odd penny. We'll have the place ready by the end of the week, move in the first lads this weekend."

Alice still thought that buying an aerocraft for cross-channel runs would have been a better investment, but couldn't deny that the money was being put to good use. It would make life so much easier for Mum, Aunt Beth, and Tom Morran.

"It's big of you, Guv, surely. And middling deedy[23]." Alice was unable hide her admiration.

---

22 Dunnamany: don't know how many. Broad Sussex idiom.
23 Deedy: clever. Broad Sussex idiom.

Chief Forty-Guts guffawed. "You remind me of myself, Alice Gunn, when I was a nipper."

"Yarr," Alice agreed. "Exceptional valour, bain't it?"

"Geemeny! No." The chief started listing: "Ill-disciplined, feral, impulsive, careless, rushing headlong for the gallows."

"Careless! Me?"

"Hatpin." He pointed at her hat. "First you blurt out a confession that you used it for wicked purposes."

Alice pouted. She had been trying to forget all about how very unclever that had been.

The chief continued. "Now, it turns out you have two hatpins. It's a bettermost trick. You had me fooled, surely. Yet, you've stuck the real one back in, knowing that you were coming to see me?"

Alice turned the hat so that the hatpins were no longer visible to him.

He sighed and turned his head to look at the gravestone again.

"Do I need to remind you, Miss Gunn, that it's a small miracle that you're standing here next to me, instead of sitting in a locked cell at the police station, waiting for the judge to send you to Lewes...or worse."

Alice gazed at the wild blue yonder overhead. There was so much of it to be seen from the churchyard's lofty elevation. Aerocraft large and small criss-crossed her vision.

"Look!" She pointed. "An old zephyr! They're a rare sight, surely!"

The chief didn't even glance up. "I owe a lot to Martha Gunn."

"Yarr, I know."

He glanced at the medal. "Your mum told you, did she?"

Alice nodded enthusiastically. "Fighting the fake French soldiers on the beach with broomsticks, bain't it? I wish I'd been there!"

The chief shook his head. "Truth is, I was terrified."

"You! You were scared?"

"We were all terrified, except Martha Gunn who wasn't afraid of the Devil himself. As far as we knew, those soldiers were real Frenchman, proper Froggies. Running down that beach, anticipating a musket volley any second…it weren't pleasant."

Alice recalled the horrors of the gunfire that night in Rottingdean. "I suppose not."

As if he had read her thoughts, the chief said: "I am genuinely sorry about what happened to your father, Alice."

Alice grew wary. She'd been enjoying their exchange more than she thought she would, but the chief had just reminded her that when all was said and done, he was a Rozzer, even if she wasn't supposed to call him that. Recalling her earlier failures to be clever at all times, she swallowed the pride of her convictions, and made to find out more first.

"Did you know my dad?"

The chief shook his head. "I saw him in passing a few times, but those were rare, all-along-of him being a fair stride away in Rottingdean. But I'd heard of him, of course, on account of his reputation. But all Lanesfolk know Clara Gunn."

"Mum! Why?"

The chief looked puzzled. "Did your parents never tell you how they met?"

"Of course, Dad had come to Brighton for the day and they met at a tea party."

"A tea party?" The chief's eyes began to twinkle with merriment, then he laughed so loud that he shook. "I suppose that's one way of putting it."

"Why? What happened?"

"Hmm, mayhap your mum had a reason to be sparse with the details."

Alice frowned. "Is it one of those things I'm not old enough to know about?"

The chief considered this before answering: "Nay. I reckon she didn't want to fill your head with notions of heroism."

"Heroism? Mum?" Forgetting that she was speaking to the Chief Constable of Brighton, Alice commanded: "You've got to tell me! I want to know."

"Mayhap your mum should be the one to tell you."

"I won't tell her," Alice promised. "I bain't a chaunter. Me lips are sealed. Cross me heart and hope to die."

The chief regarded her thoughtfully for a moment. "I suppose I've already been foolish enough to place myself in a position where I have to rely on your discretion."

Alice didn't know what he meant by that, but she agreed wholeheartedly. "You can trust me."

"I also suppose you'll hear about it sooner or later, they still sing a ballad about it in the taverns."

"A ballad? About mum?"

To Alice's surprise, the chief began to sing, in a deep baritone voice.

> *My love he is a smuggler*
> *He sails upon the sea*
> *Or chases the clouds*
> *I wish I was a smuggler*
> *For to sail along with he.*

Alice knew the song well enough, and joined in.

> *For to sail upon the sea*
> *Or skirr the blue sky*
> *For the brandy and the wine*

And to run the tubs at Shoreham
When the moon don't shine.
For the channel is his kingdom
From England down to France
And he leads the revenue cutters
In a very merry dance,

And when he comes ashore
He confounds the Excise men,
And he leaves his skiff safe moored
And comes to me again.

Alice clapped her hands. It was a good song, she'd always liked it. "That's about me mum and dad?"

"'Tis indeed," the chief confirmed. "They were a bit of a local legend."

"Why?"

"Ah. Your mum now, she was a bit of a stunner, when she were younger, reckoned to be the greatest beauty in the Lanes."

"Was she really?" Alice found it odd to think of Mum in that way. Mum had always just been Mum. It occurred to Alice that she knew very little about what Mum had been like before Dad had come along.

"Very much so. There was nary a single man in Brighton who didn't attempt to woo her, but she turned them all down."

"Except for me Dad!"

"We'll get to that bit in a moment. Now I reckon most men were relieved that she turned them down, to be honest."

Alice looked at the chief crossly. "Why? You said she was beautiful."

The chief grinned. "She were also middling deedy, like her great-grandmother Martha. Cleverer than most. Mayhap even like you. A family trait?"

"Probably," Alice agreed, somewhat mollified. "But why did that matter?"

"You'll find most men are frit of deedy women, they don't like them too clever."

Alice recalled her old school master telling her that girls shouldn't be educated too much because it would only confuse them. "Puh. Their brains are stinkibus[24]. More fool them."

"Zackly. Now when your mum was seventeen, there was much ado in Brighton. A young captain of the Yeoman Cavalry and a squadron of troopers had been sent to Hove, to help Customs & Excise take on the smugglers."

"Free Traders," Alice corrected him.

"Yarr," the chief grinned again. "Free Traders. Gentleman of the Night. Owlers. Flaskers. Or Foul Folk in the eyes of some. Criminals."

---

[24] Stinkibus: Free Trader jargon for a case of liquor left below the sea too long (an oft used hiding place for a crop) and which has subsequently gone off, no longer drinkable.

Alice shrugged. Free Traders didn't steal. They bought goods and then sold them, which is what Sussex folk had been doing since forever ago.

The chief winked, and then continued talking.

"This young captain hailed from a noble family, and like most young aristocrats he were full of himself, hot-blooded, and eager to make a name for himself. By chance, he found an informer ready to chaunt on your dad. The Free Traders had run in a crop of tea and were in the middle of landing it at Black Rock when the Yeoman Cavalry surrounded them on the beach, carbines levelled, sabres drawn."

"Rozzers," Alice hissed.

The chief ignored her interruption. "It were quite a sight, the troopers on their horses leading a sorry parade of captured Free Traders into town, followed by carts laden with bales of tea. They brought both the Free Traders and the contraband to the Town Hall, to be locked in the cells below."

"Your cells," Alice said pointedly.

"They are now," the chief agreed. "But not back then. The young captain were as proud as a peacock. Your dad's reputation was already established along the Sussex coast, so the officer had himself quite a catch. When the Free Traders were secured in the cells, the captain and most of his troopers took off to the Druid's Head to celebrate. Now it happened to be that your dad was the only Rottingdean Free Trader involved, the others were Brighton men.

Their mothers, wives, and sweethearts were plenty upset, fearing to see their menfolk dangling from the gallows before too long."

"What did they do?" Alice asked.

The chief smiled. "They did what Lanesfolk often do in times of trouble. Just like they'd once sought out Martha Gunn, this time they appealed to your grandmother and mother."

"Did mum know dad?"

"Nay, or by reputation at most. They'd never met as far as I ken. But that didn't matter to Clara Gunn, nor your granny Janet. It didn't come right to them that Brighton should be missing its men, or tea for that matter. So they made a plan. A deedy plan. Janet Gunn went about rousing the people, telling them to come to the Town Hall at midnight. Your mum, now, went to the Druid's Head."

"Where the Rozzers were!"

"Yarr, but she didn't go into the taproom, she went round the back instead. You see, the young captain not being local had no notion that the Druid's Head was run by Free Traders. Clara told them what were running the Druid's Head the Gunn plan, and they started serving the troopers undiluted spirits."

"Undiluted!" Alice was incredulous. Every child along the coast knew that spirits were run in from the sea in undiluted state, simply to save on the volume a crop took up. Once ashore, a crop had to be watered down precisely, measured carefully, before it was sold on. In undiluted state, the stuff could give the words 'dead drunk' a wholly new meaning.

"Yarr, undiluted. By midnight the young captain was still on his feet, but most of his troopers were in a stupor, or barely able to walk, let alone lift a carbine or draw a sabre. He'd left a few men at Town Hall, to support the handful of constables on duty in guarding prisoners and contraband, and those men were sober. They were also frightened when hundreds of Lanesfolk showed up, waving crow-bars, pick-axes, sledge-hammers, and pitchforks. Your granny and mum led them, armed with broomsticks."

Alice laughed, recalling Mum's remarks about the foolishness of charging things with broomsticks earlier. "Just like Great Granny Gunn!"

The chief smiled. "It seems to be the weapon of choice in your family. I dare say that a Gunn with a broom in her hands is a foe not to be underestimated. The siege of Town Hall didn't last long, its defenders took one look at the mob gathering outside and legged it. The mob broke down the front doors and then forced their way into the cells below. It were said that your dad had been put in a cell on his own, and it were your mum who unlocked the door and pulled him out."

Alice sighed dreamily. "Was that when they first kissed?"

"I don't know," the chief confessed. "If not then, somewhen soon after, all-along-of it being clear the two were head over heels. Lanesfolk called the whole affair 'The Brighton Tea Party', so in a manner of speaking, your parents did indeed meet at a tea party."

Alice laughed. It was a wonderful story. "How about the cavalry captain?"

"Captain Meadows was the laughing stock of all of Sussex the next day."

"Meadows?" Alice frowned. "The same one who was at Rottingdean?"

The chief's face fell. "Yarr. Morgan Meadows. Captain then, Colonel Meadows now."

"So he got even with dad," Alice said, a dark cloud on her face.

"I suppose he did. It didn't come right to me how he went about that business, not in the way twas done."

"He's a murderer," Alice hissed. "A murdering Rozzer."

"Now don't you go—"

"I'll get even too, learn him a thing or two," Alice promised.

"You've got some growing up to do, before you can even consider such a thing," the chief said sternly. "I want to make it absolutely clear, Alice, that my indebtedness to Martha Gunn and admiration of Clara Gunn can only stretch so far. Today's circumstances allowed for a creative interpretation of the law. But if you carry on dipping, buzzing, flimping, maltooling, smatterhauling, thimble twisting, cly faking, or stall-farming...[25]"

Alice stared at a cloudclipper, gracefully descending on its course to Hollingbury Aeroport. The chief made it sound like she was a professional pickpocket. It only happened sometimes! Like this morning, more or less by accident.

"I only–," she began to say.

"You'll be lagged[26] up in Lewes and wearing the Devil's Claws.[27] Please believe me that Lewes Prison bain't a bettermost place for a growing girl such as yourself to be."

Alice didn't need a detailed explanation. "I believe you," she said softly.

"There's more to it. I reckon I can just about get away with pulling off this convalescence home business with the Council. But there'll be folk in the Council who won't be liking me for it. If you get caught thieving and they find out, they'll force me to fire your mum and auntie."

Alice pulled a face.

---

[25] Victorian slang for specific types of pickpocketing.
[26] Lagged: locked up. Victorian slang.
[27] Broad arrows on a prison uniform. Victorian slang.

"I remember what it's like, Alice. Wheeling and dealing my way across The Lanes. I were a deedy scaddle[28], just like yourself."

"Do you remember what it's like to be frit[29] of the workhouse all the time?"

"Aye, I do. All too well. Now if you'd like to earn yourself an honest bob, somewhen–"

"I bain't going to turn chirp. I bain't a chaunter, I don't want no one paying narking dues all-along-of me[30]."

"What if I told you that I'd never ask you to chaunt on one of your own folk?"

"Quiddy?"

"I'd never ask you to whisper so much as a word to me about Lanesfolk." He gave her a sideways look and added slyly. "Nor them from Rottingdean."

"Who then? Them up Carlton Hill?" Alice asked, referring to another notorious Brighton slum.

The chief shook his head. "Posh folk. Toffs."

Alice frowned.

The chief continued, "Kemp Town, Queen's Park, Clifton Hill, Montpelier... Plenty of folk there what commit crimes. They reckon they can get away

---

[28] Scaddle: rogue. Broad Sussex idiom.
[29] Frit: afraid, frightened. Broad Sussex idiom.
[30] To turn chirp, to chaunt, to make someone pay narking dues – all related to police informers. Victorian slang.

with it. They figure that me being who I am, knowing where I came from –"

"That they can outsmart you!"

"Zackly. Somewhen, Alice, it'd benefit me to ken what folk get up to, where they go, who they visit–"

"But you got your constables for that!"

"Not enough of them to begin with. What's more, they stick out like sore thumbs. Servants now, or slum chavvies."

"They don't really see us, do they?"

"Just so. Provided the chavvy is clever about it."

"I can be clever," Alice said.

"I reckon you can be, with a bit of guidance. You need to be deedy for detective work."

Detective work!

Alice thought it over. The chief hadn't mentioned anything about Free Trading, had in fact indicated he didn't want to know, so she could still go to Uncle Yard and ask to crew. Alice Kittyhawk could be an Owler. Alice Gunn a detective. The notion of outsmarting posh folk was very tempting.

"It'd learn them Toffs a thing or two." She grinned.

"Twould," Chief Forty-Guts agreed. "There's a lady, what lives on the edge of Queen's Park now. It'd be worth a bob or two to know what she gets up to."

"She cuckolding her old man?"

The chief shook his head. "Far worse."

He gave her a meaningful look.

"Murder?!" Alice guessed, thrilled by the prospect.

"Them that ask no questions…"

Alice grinned again. Chief Forty-Guts didn't know her very well. She'd find out. She'd find out everything, know all the secrets.

"Isn't told a lie," she said. "Alright, I'll do it."

That is how Alice Kittyhawk, aka Alice Gunn, and the Chief Constable of Brighton became unlikely friends.

THE END

BONUS SHORT STORY: LIMBS

'LIMBS' was written for a writing competition in the FB group Steampunk Readers and Writers. It won second place. It's the first time Ernest Willoughby, aka Chief Forty-Guts, is introduced.

Brighton, 1870- The carriage rolled to a halt on the narrow street. A constable, wearing one of the recently introduced Bobby helmets, got off the box to open the carriage door. Ernest Willoughby, the Chief Constable of Brighton, emerged. The sixty-something-year old was tall and remarkably rotund. He had short white hair, and great, silver sideburns which partially concealed his jowls. He wore no outward badge of rank, other than his cheaply produced blue woollen police frock coat, with four ranks of dull tin buttons, some dangling dangerously loose from their threads.

Willoughby's girth had earned him the derogatory nickname 'Chief Forty-Guts', but he carried the name with pride. Fashion dictated slim and streamlined, but fashion be damned. He had learned the hard way to enjoy life when he could. More importantly, obesity was associated with a weak mind and latent mental derangement. In his line of work it was often useful to be assumed a slow and dull thinker. Being underestimated was something Willoughby enjoyed a great deal, as many had found to their misfortune.

"Here we are, sir!" The constable said.

Tim Cuffins was an impossibly young looking third-rate with an open gullible face, and an unfortunate habit of stating the obvious. "The Alfriston!"

Willoughby nodded and studied the building. The Alfriston was a hodgepodge of smaller timbered buildings amalgamated into a single one. It was tucked away amidst the winding twittens and hidden courtyards of The Lanes, the old town. In days past, the building had been a pub, run by a Free Trade gang which rivalled The Old Ship Inn and The Druid's Head in volume of illicit trade.

Willoughby grinned. Back in 1821, when the whole town had been celebrating the Coronation of George IV, the Free Traders had exploited the empty streets to move stock about in broad daylight, as bold as could be. Willoughby had earned himself a shilling clearing casks of Rhenish from The Old Ship Inn's cellars. There had been another shilling shortly after, the King's Shilling, for he had enlisted with the 35th Regiment of Foot. Drummer boy in his early teens, a Sergeant when he retired from the army forty years later. Not a scratch on him either, which was more than could be said for most of his old comrades.

He turned his focus back on The Alfriston. The building supposedly had twenty-three rooms, six staircases, thirty-eight doors, seven cellars, and untold passageways. Precisely the sort of bespoke confusion favoured by Free Traders, and Willoughby didn't doubt that some of the cellars concealed entrances to hidden tunnels.

"I shall go in alone," Willoughby declared.

Constable Cuffins made a noise that sounded like a mouse's squeak. He had been the one who had made the gruesome discovery that had brought them here.

"Sir," he said. "Wouldn't it be better to send in…there could be a mass-murderer…"

"No." Willoughby shook his head. Sending in a gaggle of excitable young policemen generally resulted in the thorough destruction of a crime scene, as well as far too many innocent bystanders being knocked about the head with truncheons, before some bright first rater decided that maybe they ought to temper their enthusiasm and ask a few questions.

He glanced at the sign over the main entrance.

Institute for Mechanickal Aggrandizement & Physickal Recouperation

There wasn't a great deal that couldn't be solved by an amiable chat, even in ghastly cases such as this one appeared to be, to judge by the grisly account provided by Constable Cuffins. It had even unsettled Willoughby, who was not easily troubled. The carnage of untold battlefields in the everlasting wars with France had seen to that. It made most domestic murders seem tranquil affairs of little consequence.

Ignoring the anchor-shaped iron door knocker, Willoughby tried the handle. Upon finding the door unlocked, he swung it open and entered.

He found himself in a small hallway, with doors to either side, and a cloak room in front of him. The broadcloth frock coats neatly arrayed behind the mahogany counter were somber blacks and dark greys of fine quality. Some variety was provided by a few tweed country coats, and a single scarlet army coat with gold piping and epaulettes, an officer of the 35th, Willoughby's old regiment.

"Here be gentlemen," Willoughby muttered unhappily.

"Now there bain't naun reason for ye to be spying and eying these here bettermost coats." A cloak room attendant emerged from a dark nook. He was tall and broad-shouldered, with brown sideburns, and small, mean eyes. "Go cut yer stick and be gone…Oh!"

"My stick?" Willoughby let his coat fall open, to reveal the stout truncheon suspended from the belt around his elephantine waist.

"Begging yer pardon, sir." The man spoke with wary respect. "Do ye got an appointment?"

He gestured at one of the doors, which was all that Willoughby required of him.

"None of your bloody business," he growled at the man, and then opened the indicated door to enter a parlour suggestive of a gentlemen's club. A few gents occupied some of the gilded velvet chairs, all reading newspapers or staring intently at gold-lettered brochures. Their colourful silk waistcoats were festooned with cog & gear broches, and pins made of silver and gold.

Incongruously, they were wearing their top hats indoors. All of the hats sported fanciful arrangements of feathers and gleaming brass goggles with darkened lenses.

"Hell's bells," Willoughby muttered. As an infantryman he had a healthy disdain of both cavalry and airmen. It was well known that the former let their horses do the thinking, and the latter their nether-regions. The Chief Constable disapproved strongly of the contemporary fashion of the better classes. If appearances were to be believed, more than half of England's gentry were intrepid aerial adventurers these days.

"I thought this was supposed to be a quality establishment," one of the gentlemen said softly, but loud enough for Willoughby to hear.

The Chief Constable ignored him. He picked up one of the brochures, letting his eyes roam over the cream paper, pausing only briefly at formulations such as "commutation of appurtenances" and "addendum of augmented extremities."

Things were beginning to make sense. Willoughby recalled Cuffins's distraught report, of the barrels spotted over a courtyard wall, their macabre contents drawing a great buzz of flies, and only a net spread over the courtyard keeping shrieking seagulls at bay.

An orderly, dressed entirely in white, entered the room, his eyes gliding over the gentlemen to assess any possible needs. He frowned concern when he spotted Willoughby.

"May I be of assistance…?"

"I'd like to speak to the manager of this establishment," Willoughby answered.

"Dr Dryden?!" The orderly raised his eyebrows. "I am afraid the doctor is far too busy…perhaps you could make an appointment…"

Willoughby shrugged. He had tried to be nice, now he would employ more traditional police methods. He slid his truncheon out of its leather scabbard, and casually swept it around in half a circle, knocking a Chinese vase off its mahogany stand. The fancy vase broke into smithereens on the fine Turkish carpet. Some of the gentlemen looked in his direction, before turning their eyes back to their reading material.

"Oops-a-daisy." The apology in Willoughby's tone was contrasted by the steel glare in his eyes.

"I will make your presence known to Dr Dryden at once," the orderly said, before rushing out of the waiting room.

"Boorish lout." One of the gents muttered his disapproval.

"Forty-Guts," one whispered to a comrade, the speaker a young man with the bold – but foolish – audacity of youth.

Willoughby still had his truncheon in his hand and tapped it meaningfully on the sidetable by the young man's chair. The man paled.

"*Chief* Forty-Guts to you," Willoughby growled, and then made for the door through which the orderly had exited. He had no intention of waiting patiently.

Wandering through the Alfriston was as confusing as he had feared, it really was a maze. He stumbled upon a ward. The beds were occupied by pale patients, all were missing limbs, their arm or leg stumps carefully bandaged.

"Tarnation," Willoughby uttered softly. Even though there were no signs of blood or battle stains, it was as if he had walked in on a poignant scene from his past. Visits to crude field hospitals to speak words of encouragement to stricken comrades, trying to smile and jest, and not think too much of their severed limbs piled up outside the surgery tents, nor acknowledge the foul smell of gangrene.

He withdrew from the door opening, feeling empathy for the patients, and then continued his tour. The case was as good as solved, but there were still a few loose ends. He found another ward, but the patients here looked snug and smug, most of them wearing those damned decorated top hats, all invested with excited energy as they marvelled at themselves.

Willoughby stared. He had seen a few of the contraptions on the streets, but always mere glimpses in passing. Arms, legs–replaced by steel frames, small pistons, whirring gears, brass encasings, leather tendons.

"Damn my eyes!" Willoughby shook his head in disbelief.

"Upon my soul! Sergeant Willoughby!" One of the patients with a mechanical contraption replacing an arm called out.

Old habits die hard. Willoughby snapped to attention and saluted. "Captain Griffiths, sir!"

"At ease, Sergeant. It's Major Griffiths now," the man said, modest pride on his friendly face. He moved his mechanical arm. It hissed, blowing out a few miniature plumes of smoke, but the movement was clumsy and awkward.

"Well," Griffiths demanded. "What do you think of it? I still have to get used to it, but I shall have full control before too long."

"Were you wounded, sir?" Willoughby followed news from his old regiment but hadn't been aware of any recent fighting.

"Wounded?! Good Lord! No, not at all." Major Griffiths raised his artificial upper arm and stared at it with delight. "I shall be the envy of the Officer's Mess, don't you think so?"

"The envy…?" Willoughby was appalled.

"One couldn't be more fashionable if one tried," Griffiths confirmed. "Although perhaps I shouldn't expect a man of your station to…"

"Yes, sir," Willoughby said. "No, sir."

He kept his face impassive but thought of old comrades from the 35th. Wearing their faded and frayed red coats, thrusting out their battlefield stumps on the streets in the hope of eliciting enough pity to merit a charitable ha'penny.

A new voice spoke. "Alas! This is most unfortunate!"

Willoughby turned around to see a young man in his thirties entering the ward, black-haired with a square jaw and an impeccable moustache. He was wearing a white coat. A stethoscope dangled from his neck.

"Doctor Justin Dryden," the man introduced himself, but didn't extend a hand. Instead, he frowned. "It is of the utmost importance that my patients are left undisturbed, Inspector."

"Chief Constable." Willoughby corrected him.

The doctor shrugged indifferently. "I can assure you, that we run a legitimate operation."

Willoughby raised his eyebrows. He doubted a legitimate operation would set up shop in The Lanes.

Dr Dryden hastily added: "There is no unnatural enhancement."

"Unnatural enhancement?"

"Forbidden by law." The doctor's renewed frown suggested that Willoughby should have known this. He pointed at Major Griffith's mechanical arm. "These contraptions are perfect imitations of human limbs, mirroring strength and dexterity, but no more than that, nothing to give the patient any physical advantage…"

Then what on earth are they good for? Willoughby wondered, but he already had an answer to that. *Fashion*…he scowled.

"I've come about a matter of public health, Doctor."

"I can assure you–"

"No, you can't." Willoughby abandoned the ward, striding down a corridor, hoping he was guessing the building's interior layout correctly.

"Wait! You cannot…" Dr Dryden scurried after him.

Willoughby threw open a door and marched through an operating room, past a steel surgery table, and an array of tourniquets, scalpels, knives, capital saws, and artery forceps waiting on metal trays. He opened a door at the far end of the room, letting in a cascade of daylight, as well as a putrid stench.

The Chief Constable stood in the doorway, staring at the sight which had caused Cuffins to suspect the presence of a mass murderer in The Alfriston. A scene evoking memories…the rasp of steel sawing through bones, spine-chilling screams, eyes haunted by pain, eyes sightless in death…

The doctor caught up with him.

"This ain't seemly," Willoughby indicated the open barrels from which protruded blood-spattered, amputated human limbs, in various stages of decay.

"It's standard procedure…"

Willoughby gathered two fistfuls of white coat and pulled Dr Dryden close enough to smell the man's breath. "It don't come right to me. It scares folks and can't be healthy. You'll see to the proper disposal of these…things. Or would you like me to develop a keen interest in the specifics of unnatural enhancement?"

He saw worry flash in the doctor's eyes.

"We'll dispose of them," Dr Dryden agreed.

"Good." Willoughby let go of the man, turned, and walked away. He was disgusted, haunted by vivid memories, and eager to get back to the sanity of burglaries, robberies and the occasional domestic murder. Fashion be damned.

THE END

HISTORICAL NOTES ON MARTHA GUNN, THE BATTLE OF THE BROOMSTICKS, AND THE BRIGHTON TEA PARTY

Martha Gunn as depicted on the 'Portrait of Martha Gunn' (1795) by John Russel.

Martha Gunn existed. Her grave can be visited at St Nicholas Church in Brighton. She was quite a character, and indeed friends of sorts with 'Prinny'.

I am indebted to military historian and author Roy Christopher Grant, who dedicated some time I had no right to claim to help me get to the bottom of the incident I have called 'The Battle of the Broomsticks.'

It is most well-known from the illustration by John Colley Nixon in 1794, showing Martha Gunn and other women beating back a "French" invasion of Brighton. Its intention was to deliver satirical comment on the lack of preparedness for a French invasion.

Part of John Colley Nixon's satirical print. I found this copy at the Brighton Fishing Museum on the city's seafront (well worth a visit).

However, it's likely that Nixon based it on an actual incident. In his *The Brighton Garrison*, Roy Christopher Grant relates that the 'battle' took place during Easter exercises near Brighton. The Prince Regent, fond of pageantry and military re-enactment, had organised a mock invasion of Brighton by British troops dressed as French soldiers. These troops hailed from the north of England, possibly Northumbria. Grant told me "some locals heard them speaking in a funny dialect, assumed they were French, and a battle ensued."

Grant points out that the two men hiding in the bathing machines (not visible above) were caricatures of the two British Generals Sheridan and Fox, "who were fully aware that the 'invaders' weren't French and were much amused by the whole event".

I placed this battle a few decades later to be able to fit in Sergeant Ernest Willoughby as a young boy. I don't know if this was indeed the first time the Prince Regent and Martha Gunn met, nor do we know for sure she participated in the 'battle'. That said, I find it hard to believe that such a prominent Brighton character would have missed out on the fun, and she certainly would have been noticed by 'Prinny' had she been there. The medal is an invention. Whatever else, I believe that this incident is a magnificent example of the 'We Wunt Be Druv' stubbornness and independent streak that marks Sussex.

"Get thee back to France!"

As for the Brighton Tea Party, this is entirely fictional. However, there are numerous accounts from across the British Isles, from Kent to Scotland and doubling back to Cornwall, of mobs of angry women liberating confiscated contraband from the authorities, and also 'un-arresting' their captured menfolk.

The story of Clara Gunn and John Hawkeye is based on an incident in Dover in 1820, when an angry crowd not only released captured smugglers from the town jail, but also proceeded to tear the building apart, using the rooftiles and bricks to pelt the authorities with as the smugglers made their escape.

A broadside at the time described how the mob:

"commenced an attack on the gaol with crow-bars, pick-axes, hammers, saws &c &c, unroofed the top, and threw part of the side wall down, and, not only released the whole of the eleven smugglers, but several other prisoners confined in the gaol under sentence, and they succeeded in getting them clear off."

NOTES ON ALICE

Alice Kittyhawk, aka Alice Gunn, aka Liss Hawkeye is the central character of:

Sussex Steampunk Tales,

Steam Smugglers of Southshire,

The Time Flight Chronicles.

Image of 'Alice Kittyhawk' by photographer Heijo Van De Werf. This image was used for the cover of Rottingdean Rhyme and the same model features (or will feature) on the covers of Them that Ask No Questions, Fair Weather for Foul Folk, and Sussex Rising! The model's first name, I was delighted to discover, is Alice.

Alice's story starts with the *Sussex Steampunk Tale* novella *Rottingdean Rhyme*, which was originally written as *The Rottingdean Rhyme* for the Writerpunk Press anthology: *What We've Unlearned, English Class goes Punk*.

It continues with various *Steam Smugglers of Southshire* stories, a collaborative effort with Daren Callow's *Tales of New Albion* podcasts. The first story in this series is entitled: *A Sea Voyage on Wheels*.

Within the *Sussex Steampunk Tales* series, this novella, *Them that Ask no Questions*, picks up where *Rottingdean Rhyme* left off, and is to be followed by the novella *Fair Weather for Foul Folk*, set in Hastings & Rye.

Further short stories will follow in various anthologies in 2019/2020 including *Jewels From the Deep*, *The Skirring Dutchman*, *Sussex by the Sea*, and *Secrets of the Seven Sisters*.

Longer works are planned or already in progress, including the novella *Fair Weather for Foul Folk*, and the novels: *For the Love of a Republic: Sussex Rising!* and *For the Love of a Republic: The Rock-a-Nore Murders*.

All the stories can be read as stand-alone stories, or else as part of a series.

The *Time Flight Chronicles*, of which the first book *Amster Damned* was published a few years ago, follow Alice as an adult and private investigator who gets embroiled in temporal displacement in search of her childhood friend Dr Braxton Beesworth.

Further information can be found on www.nilsnissevisser.co.uk

Older Alice. Picture by Jack Savage.
Model Amelia Anna.

ABOUT THE AUTHOR

I was born in Rotterdam in 1970. I've lived in The Netherlands, Thailand, Nepal, Oklahoma (USA), Tanzania, the United Kingdom, Egypt, & France. I currently reside in Brighton, Sussex, although I like to claim I moved into my imagination full-time after having been told I spend too much time there once too often. I still haven't paid my Poll Tax and hope to become a pirate when I grow up.

After five years of writing non-fiction for magazines around the world, I self-published my debut novel (Escape from Neverland) in 2014. Ten novels and novellas later, as well as over a dozen short stories published in international anthologies, and there is no end in sight yet. My great-grandfather's cousin Piet Visser wrote twenty-one books, a number that obviously needs to be equalled or surpassed. Somewhat socially awkward, I don't understand the purpose of idle chit-chat, but can be triggered into speaking about books, archery, pirates, smugglers, steampunk, animal rescues, homelessness issues, or my love of Sussex.

I promise to chant your name to the full moon on top of Hollingbury Camp if you write me a nice review.

Special thanks to Janet Going, Carol Gyzander, and Rowan Potter for providing feedback during writing.

ABOUT THE PHOTOGRAPHER

I have been working with Corin Spinks since 2014. He's Sussex born, so as stubborn as a goat and never does entirely what I ask of him. I kindly forgive him for assuming to know more about of his area of expertise than I do (cause I sometimes take a snap shot with my phone camera, you know, which makes me quite the photographer), simply because the results are always stunningly magnificent (especially considering that my sagely advice has been partially ignored).

Corin has done many of my covers, as well as promo-shots, and invaluable help with local homeless projects in Brighton. He also contributes to the stories by sending me images out of the blue, challenging me to write them into stories. About half the characters in *Amster Damned*, as well as some crucial plot elements, resulted from impromptu, unplanned input by Corin.

Over the last five years it's been a pleasure to see a growing appreciation of Corin's work, as well as increasing professional recognition.

Check out his work here:

www.flickr.com/photos/corinography

THE RAGGED VICTORIANS, THE GREAT UNWASHED

The "Ragged Victorians - The Great Unwashed" are an award-winning living history group, re-enacting the lower classes of Victorian England c1851.

Their work is incredible. I cannot begin to describe how much I admire them and how much inspiration they provide, especially since (you may have noted) I'm of mind Victorian Times were far more than gentlefolk having jolly japes.

I must add that my interpretation of the Brighton Constabulary at this time is entirely my own, driven by narrative needs and my hope to base as much as possible on hard facts, rather than seeking exact historical representation. Any mistakes, major or minor, are mine, and do not reflect the superb background research conducted by the Ragged Victorians.

www.raggedvictorians.co.uk